THE CASE OF THE BLACK-HOODED HANGMANS

THE CASE OF THE
BLACK-HOODED HANGMANS

John R. Erickson

Illustrations by Gerald L. Holmes

Maverick Books
Published by Gulf Publishing Company
Houston, Texas

Maverick Books
Published by Gulf Publishing Company
P. O. Box 2608, Houston, Texas 77252-2608

10 9 8 7 6 5 4 3 2 1

Library of Congress Cataloging-in-Publication Data

Erickson, John R., 1943–
    The case of the black-hooded hangmans / John R. Erickson ;
illustrations by Gerald L. Holmes.
      p. cm. — (Hank the Cowdog ; 24)
    Summary: When he gets blamed after one of Eddy the
raccoon's tricks backfires, Hank's search for the missing Eddy
leads him and his sidekick Drover to a haunted house.
    ISBN 0-87719-267-7. — ISBN 0-87719-266-9 (pbk.). — ISBN
0-87719-268-5 (cassette)
    1. Dogs—West (U.S.)—Fiction. [1. Dogs—Fiction. 2. Ranch life—
West (U.S.) —Fiction. 3. West (U.S.)—Fiction. 4. Humorous stories.
5. Mystery and detective stories.]   I. Holmes, Gerald L., ill.   II. Title.
III. Series: Erickson, John R., 1943–   Hank the Cowdog ; 24.
PS3555.R428C35   1995
813'.54—dc20   94-48713
                                                CIP
                                                AC

Printed in the United States of America.

iv

To my favorite newlyweds,
Scot and Tiffany Erickson

C O N T E N T S

C H A P T E R

1

IF A FLY CAN FLEE, CAN A FLEA FLY?

It's me again, Hank the Cowdog. Do you remember Eddy the raccoon? We called him Eddy the Rac for short, and he caused nothing but trouble from the first day he arrived on the ranch.

He was an orphan, see. His ma got run over on the county road. Slim the Cowboy found him up in a tree and took him home to raise.

I knew that was a bad idea. I could have told 'em but nobody asked my opinion. Who am I, after all? I'm merely the Head of Ranch Security, the guy who runs this ranch day after day and night after night, the guy who puts his life on the line to protect it from monsters and so forth.

And from coons, who are very destructive. If you want the inside story on coons, ask a Head of

1

Ranch Security. If not for us, the coons would have taken over years ago. They would have stolen all the feed out of the feed barn, all the machines out of the machine shed, and all the corn out of the corn patch.

Oh yes, and all the eggs out of the chicken house, but that happens to be a sensitive subject and I'm not sure I want to talk about it.

Yes, I'd had lots of experience in dealing with Eddy's kinfolks, and I knew for a fact that coons weren't nice guys. But what was I supposed to do when Slim brought Eddy home and decided to make a pet of him?

All at once we had this little con artist on the place and I had strict orders to be nice to him. Okay, so I went out of my way to be nice to him. What did it get me? You'll see.

But I'll give you a little hint. It was Eddy who led us to the Haunted House which happened to be full of . . . I don't want to scare anybody, so hang on.

Maybe I shouldn't even mention it. It's too scary.

Oh, maybe you can handle it. We'll give it a shot. It was full of BLACK-HOODED HANGMANS! Pretty scary, huh? I warned you.

Anyways, where were we? I guess it was in the winter, late January or early February. It was cold and snowy. Gloomy weather. Eddy had been living with us for several months, as I recall, and had broken all records for making mischief.

See, he had a real talent for thinking up mischief and luring me into his schemes. Then, after the mischief was done, he would disappear, and guess who always got caught. And blamed. And yelled at and scolded.

Me.

Well, you can fool Hank the Cowdog once in a row and you can also fool him twice in a row, if you're pretty clever, and sometimes even four or five times in a row.

Maybe that's hard for you to believe, that a rinky-dink little raccoon could fool the Head of Ranch Security many times in a row. I'm sorry to disappoint you, but he did. I admit it.

But let me hasten to add that I had learned valuable lessons on the subject of coons:

1. Never believe anything a coon tells you.
2. Never take advice from one.
3. And above all, never ever help one escape from his cage in the middle of the night.

Yes, I had been to school on coons, and the experience had made me a stronger, wiser, more mature dog. The chances that I would ever be fooled again by a raccoon had shrunk down to zero, or below zero.

All right, so it was a brittle cold evening towards the end of January. Eddy the Rac was camped in his cage in front of the machine shed, and as I recall, he was asleep.

Yes, of course he was because that's typical coon behavior. They fall asleep around six o'clock in the evening, and then when everybody else is ready to hit the gunnysack, they're wide awake and ready to play.

Eddy was racked out. A little play on words there. Get it? Eddy the Rac was *racked out,* which means asleep. Pretty good, huh? I get a kick out of . . .

What was I talking about? Oh yes, cornbread. Sally May had pitched out a few slices of week-old cornbread with the evening scraps. Drover and I raced for them, and naturally, I won.

I won the cornbread and then proceeded to . . . well, choke and cough, if you must know the truth. Cornbread is very dry. Week-old cornbread is even drier than fresh. I wolfed it down, just as I might have gobbled meat or regular bread or any one of your other food groups.

Wolfing cornbread is a bad idea. Never wolf cornbread. It's made of tiny particles, don't you see, and they are dry and they can get caught in your . . . whatever.

Your windbag. Your breathing pore. The hole your air goes through when you take a breath. We call it the *Coffus Makus* for reasons which are too complicated to explain.

Oh well, I'll try, even though it's very very technical and scientific. See, in Security Work we have to use a lot of technical terms. Your ordinary dogs can't handle the big words and the huge concepts, so they rarely use them.

Heads of Ranch Security, on the other hand . . .

How did we get on the subject of cornbread? I thought we were discussing raccoons.

Hmmmm. Very strange.

I mean, once I get locked in on a subject matter, I'm like a heat-seeking guided mistletoe. I go straight to the target and virtually destroy it in a blaze of wit and logic and so forth, and very seldom do I get distracted from my primary mission.

Your ordinary run of mutts have a hard time finishing a sentence or completing a thought. Too many distractions. Drover is a perfect example. His mind is always wandering: to the clouds, to a butterfly, to a flea crawling around on his . . .

You won't believe this, but at this very moment, I mean, even as we speak, a flea is crawling around on my . . . tee hee . . . crawling up my left hind leg. It tickles. I mean, it REALLY tickles, and if it weren't for Iron Discipline, I would probably . . .

Hee hee, ha ha, ho ho!

We're talking about Serious Tickles here, fellers, and I may have to break off in a minute and go to Countermeasures. I'd rather not because I want to finish the business about the cornbread, and once I've opened up a subject for discussion, I hate to . . .

Ho! Hee! Ha!

This is tough, but let me try to mush on. See, I gobbled down the cornbread and I can't stand this any more. I've got to do something about that stupid flea.

Hang on.

I'll be right back.

Chew chew chew!
Gnaw gnaw gnaw!
Bite bite bite!
Chew gnaw bite!
Gnaw bite chew!
Chew bite gnaw!

Ahhhhhhhhhhhhh!

Say goodbye to the flea, for he hath gone to the place where fleas go when they have messed around with the wrong dog.

I hate fleas. Fleas and flies. They're worthless and they drive me nuts.

G.L. Holmes

What Good Is A Flea Or A Fly?

What good is a flea or a fly?
What good is a fly or a flea?
If you flick at a fly, it will try to flee,
If you flick at a flea, it will try to fly,
But won't.

See, a fly can flee, 'cause a fly can fly,
'Cause a fly has wings and that is why
A fly can flee as well as fly,
But a flea can only try to fly.
Whatever.

A flea can hop or hope to fly,
A fly can fly or hope to hop,
But neither can do them both at
   once,
And I can't tell you why.
Don't you see?

If a fly can fly and a flea can flee,
You'd think that a flea could fly.
Well, maybe it can, I'm getting
   confused,
And who really cares? Not me.
Goodbye.

Pretty good, huh? I get a kick out of messing around with words and poetry and stuff, and you'll be proud to know that I got rid of the flea, which brings us back to the important subject we were . . .

What were we discussing? Huh. It just vanished. Had it right on the tip of my tongue, so to speak, but then . . .

The sunset? Maybe that was it. We had a pretty sunset that evening. We have one every evening but some are prettier than others. This one had lots of pink and orange in it, but that's not what we were talking about.

Hang on, I'll get it here in a second.

I hate it when this happens.

Okay, I've got it now. Cornbread. Drover and I raced for the cornbread and I won, little suspecting that it would come very near to choking me to death. I coughed and harked and wheezed, and finally managed to . . .

Eddy the Rac. Forget the stupid cornbread, also the fleas and flies. I don't know how you got me talking about those things anyway. Somehow you managed to distract me and I wish you wouldn't do that.

It makes me look silly, and nothing could be further from the truth. I'm not silly at all. I'm a very serious dog. That's why you rarely see me smiling, because I rarely smile, because life is very serious.

And if life is very serious, what's left to smile about? Not much. You think about that whilst I try to get organized.

Coming up: Eddy the Rac. Never mind the cornbread.

C H A P T E R
2
CAUTION: TOXIC SAWDUST CORNBREAD

Okay, here we go.

It was a warm, lazy evening in August. Drover and I were down at the gas tanks, lounging on our gunnysack beds and more or less killing time.

Hold on. It was a cold brittle evening in February. Now we're cooking.

Lounging and killing time aren't things I do very often. Drover does it all the time because . . . well, he's a fairly boring personality and more than slightly inclined to be lazy.

Anyways, for a brief span of time, I found myself killing time. Or to put it another way, I was catching a few moments of rest before darkness fell and I had to go back out on Night Patrol.

Drover had his ears folded back and was looking up at the clouds. I know it was foolish of me, but on a sudden impulse, I said, "A penny for your thoughts, Drover."

"Oh, it's fine. How's yours?"

"Pretty good. It's been better but it's been worse." There was a moment of silence. "What are we talking about?"

He gave me his usual blank stare. "Your appendix."

"My appendix? Why would you ask about my appendix?"

"I don't know. You asked about mine and I thought I'd be nice and ask about yours, and I did and you said yours was pretty good. I'm glad it's better."

"Thanks. Yes, it's much better." There was another moment of silence. "When did I ask about your appendix?"

"Oh, I don't know. Sometime."

"Be more specific please. Yesterday? Today? Tomorrow?"

He twisted his mouth around and scowled. "Well, it wasn't tomorrow. And I don't think it was yesterday. Maybe it was today."

"All right, now we're getting somewhere. Let's see if we can narrow it down a little more. What time today?"

"Well, let's see. I don't remember."

"Drover!"

"Let me think. Okay, I think I've got it now. It was just a little while ago."

"You mean this evening, just now?"

"Yep, I'm almost sure it was."

I shook my head. "Drover, what I said was, a penny for your thoughts."

"I'll be derned. I thought you asked about my appendix."

"No. I did not ask about your appendix."

"I'll be derned. I guess I heard the penny part and thought it was appendix instead of a penny."

"Yes, it certainly appears that's what you thought, but that's not what I said."

"I guess not."

"In the first place, I don't care about your appendix. In the second place, I'm not sure that dogs even have one. In the third place, you're wasting my valuable time."

"Sorry. I thought I had one."

"You don't have one."

"Then how come it hurts all the time?"

I glared at the runt. "If you don't have one, it can't hurt."

"No fooling? Gosh, I feel better already."

"Good. I'm feeling slightly insane."

"'Course, this old leg still gives me fits. Maybe it was the leg all the time."

"It's been a leg for years, Drover, the very same leg you've always had."

"I guess you're right. Gosh, I feel great, Hank. Thanks a million."

Sometimes . . . oh well.

At that very moment I was rescued from the swamp of Drover's mind by the slamming of the screen door up at the house. My ears shot up. My eyebrows shot up. My mouth began to water. New meaning surged into my life. I leaped to my feet.

Drover had heard it too, and he leaped to his feet. "Scraps!"

"Hey Drover, a penny for your thoughts."

"A whole penny? Oh boy! Well, let's see here . . . "

ZOOM!

I went streaking up to the yard gate and, heh heh, was first in line for the alleged scraps. I wagged my tail and gave Sally May my most charming smile.

Her gaze went past me. "Where's Drover?"

Who? Oh, him. How should I know? Goofing off somewhere and he probably wasn't hungry anyway. I was pretty sure that he wouldn't mind if I ate his share of the, uh, scraps.

She scraped the plate, and it's funny how the sound of that fork scraping over the plate causes my mouth to . . . gurgle, slurp, drip . . . causes my mouth to water.

It also gives me a powerful urge to dive onto the scraps and wolf them down before . . . well, before they can dry up or get stale, so to speak.

And I did dive onto the scraps and I did wolf . . .

COUGH, COUGH! HARK, ULP, ARG!

Cornbread. Dry cornbread.

Were you aware that at certain stages in its growth and development, cornbread can be poisonous and very dangerous? It can be. I learned this through bitter experience, when I came very close to strangulating right there in front of Sally May.

Do you know what she said? She said, and this is a direct quote, she said, "Well, Mister Greedy McPig, if you'd chew your food, instead of gulping it down, maybe you wouldn't strangle yourself."

It had nothing to do with gulping or being greedy. It was her cornbread recipe. I happen to know that you're supposed to put some kind of moisture into cornbread—milk, eggs, shortening, stuff like that. I mean, nobody can eat cornbread that's as dry as . . . something. Horse feed. Sand. Sawdust.

G.L. Holmes

No wonder she threw it out. It would have choked a horse. It's just a shame that she didn't label it for what it was—poisonous and toxic material.

Suppose I had choked to death right there in front of her. Imagine the terrible guilt she would have felt, and I mean for the rest of her life. Terrible burden.

15

One of the sad facts that we dogs must live with is that our human friends will slip us any kind of rubbish and garbage. I mean, they mess up the recipe and come up with something THEY can't chew and THEY can't swallow and THEY can't stand to keep in their mouths, and what do they do with it?

Give it to the dogs.

Right. As though we spend the whole day just waiting for the next batch of burned toast, incinerated cookies, moldy ham, and sawdust cornbread.

And they actually expect us to eat the stuff!

The strange part of all this is that . . . hmmm, we usually do, which makes you wonder . . .

That's about all the time we have to spend on Toxic Sawdust Cornbread.

The important point to remember is that I survived the ordeal, no thanks to Sally May, and became a much wiser dog.

Just as I had passed through this dangerous spell of coughing and choking, Drover came padding up from the gas tanks.

"Hi Hank. You owe me a penny."

"A penny for what?"

"You said you'd give me a penny for my thoughts."

"Oh yes, so I did. Unfortunately, I had an emergency call and wasn't able to hear all your thoughts. I'm sure I missed out on something very special."

"Oh yeah, it was pretty exciting. I came up with three whole thoughts."

"No kidding? Do I dare ask what they were?"

"Oh sure, I'd love to tell you . . . if I can remember. Gosh, I hope I haven't lost 'em."

"Yes, that would be a tragedy."

"Let me see here." He screwed his face into a knot and rolled his eyes around. "Okay, here we go. Thought Number One: No one knows more about being a fly than a fly."

I stared into the huge vacuum of his eyes. "That's a thought?"

"Yeah, you like it?"

"I . . . it leaves me speechless, Drover."

"Gosh, thanks."

"What's the next one?"

"The next one. Let's see here. Thought Number Two: There's a pot of rainwater at the end of every rainbow."

"Uh huh, not bad. Let's move on to Number Three."

"Okay. Thought Number Three." His eyes went blank, even more blank than they were before. "Gosh, I can't remember. I've lost it."

"That's too bad, son. I was really looking forward to hearing it."

"Yeah, me too, 'cause it was a wonderful thought, the best one I ever came up with."

"That's a real tragedy, Drover, but of course I can't possibly pay you a penny for only two thoughts."

"Oh darn! Now I'm really sad and upset. It almost breaks my heart, 'cause I tried so hard and worked so hard."

"Yes, I see what you mean. And what really makes it sad is that those may have been the only three thoughts you ever came up with in a single day, and I mean in your whole life."

"Yeah." He was almost in tears now. "They were my very best and I was so proud of myself!"

I patted the little mutt on the shoulder and tried to comfort him in his hour of greatest need.

"Drover, this is a very sad moment and I feel that I should do something to reward you for your effort."

You'll never guess what he got as his reward.

C H A P T E R

3

DROVER'S REWARD AND THE ULTRA-CRYPTO SECRET CODE

Drover's eyes brightened and a grin spread across his mouth. "Really? A reward, no fooling? Oh, that would be so kind!"

"Yes, well . . . there's more to me than steel and iron and steel, Drover."

"You said steel twice."

"Do you want a reward or not?"

"Sorry."

"Never correct your superiors. Okay, here's my best offer. I can't give you a penny for two thoughts. I'm afraid it would corrupt you in small but insignificant ways. But to show you how proud I am, I'm going to give you the rest of the evening scraps."

19

His eyes went to the cornbread on the ground. "A cake of sawdust?"

"It's Sally May's cornbread, Drover, and I can't tell you how delicious it is. You may have the rest of it. Congratulations."

I watched with, uh, great interest as he pounced upon the cornbread and wolfed it down.

He didn't choke.

He didn't even cough. The little dunce. I couldn't believe it.

He swallowed the last bite and gave me this big stupid grin. "Thanks, Hank. Cornbread beats a penny any day."

"Shut up, Drover. You take a good idea and run it straight into the ground."

Darkness had fallen and it was time for me to begin my Night Patrol, which is one of my most important jobs on this outfit. Even though Drover had made a fool of himself by eating inedible food products, I decided to give him another chance.

I assigned him the job of checking out the Eastern Quadrant of ranch headquarters. We divide up the headquarters area into five quadrants, don't you see, and the EQ (that's our code name for Eastern Quadrant), the EQ is the least likely of all of them to attract troublemakers.

I gave Drover the EQ and I took ATOQ. That's another code word and maybe I shouldn't reveal what it means. There is some danger in revealing our codes. I'm sure you understand. See, if our codes fell into the wrong hands, there's no telling what might happen, but it would be serious.

Very serious. I mean, the safety of our agents might be in jepperdee . . . japperdee . . . jepordie . . . might be in danger, grave danger.

There's nothing personal in this, so don't get your feelings hurt. I'm under strict orders not to reveal any more of our . . . oh what the heck, it probably won't hurt to declassify one little code word.

But only on the condition that you promise never to blab these code words to a coon, coyote, skunk, badger, fiend, phantom, or monster.

Promise?

Okay. (Make sure no one's looking.) All set? (And don't forget that you promised.) Here we go.

The Code Decryption Procedure
Will Now Begin

WHAT YOU ARE ABOUT TO WITNESS HERE, BEFORE YOUR VERY EYES, IS THE TRANSMISSION OF TOP-SECRET, HIGHLY CLASSIFIED INFORMATION IN ULTRA-CRYPTO CODE.

YOU SHOULD BE WARNED THAT THIS INFORMATION IS SO DREADFULLY SECRET THAT IT SOMETIMES CAUSES DIAPER RASH ON EXPOSED SKIN.

IT HAS ALSO BEEN LINKED TO HEART-BURN, CELERY WILTAGE, AND CERTAIN FORMS OF RINGWORM. YOU ARE URGED TO TAKE ALL SAFETY PRECAUTIONS.

The Code Decryption Program Has Begun
Decryption Procedure In Progress
Please Hold
Joe's Grill Has The Best Burgers In Town
Install Safety Devices Now
Hi, We're Away From The Phone Right Now
And . . .
Disregard Previous Message
Prepare Visual Devices To See Decrypted Code
Stand By!
Three . . .
Two . . .
One . . .
Two . . .
Three . . .
Seventeen . . .
Four and Twenty Blackbirds Baked In A Pie
Warning! Disk Full

Drive Slow, Old Cats

Burp

Have A Good Day Good Day Good Day
Good Day

SYSTEM FAILURE!!

@#$%&*^%%$#@**&^%%$#@!@##$

Okay, we seem to be having a little trouble with Data Control. Those things happen every once in a while. Sorry, I guess we can't decode the secret message.

I hate that.

On the other hand, do you suppose that we could do it manually? Why not? Hang on a second. We'll switch everything over to Manual—here, here, and here—and we'll see if we can do the decoding by hand.

I think this might work.

Stand by.

Okay, here we go.

> EQ is the code word for "Eastern
>   Quadrant."
>
> ATOQ is the code word for "All
>   The Other Quadrants."

Hey, all right, we did it! Pretty good for a ranch dog, huh? You bet it is.

Well, that was a lot of trouble but it was worth it. It gives you a little glimpse into the shadowy world we inhabit in the Security Business, a world of spies, secrets, treachery, and high-tech adventure.

Anyways, it was time for Night Patrol, and you now have enough information to know where I was going on this mission. I steamed down to the corrals, did a QVS of the feed barn, the sick pen, the wire lot, and the saddle shed.

Sorry, QVS means "Quick Visual Scan." More code. I know it's pretty complicated but just bear with me.

From there, I cut a ninety (made a ninety-degree turn) and proceeded on a new course, bearing 806-435-7611 degrees of lingerie (straight east). This took me past Emerald Pond, through the grove of elm trees, past the gas tanks, up the hill, through the snow, and up to the machine shed.

The patrol had left me near exhaustion. I mean, you can't imagine the amount of energy it takes to remember all the procedures, go back and forth through our various codes, and maintain a high level of alertness.

You probably thought a Night Patrol was a simple deal, the kind of thing any dog could do. Now you know the truth.

Where was I? Oh yes, in front of the machine shed, exhausted but warmed by the inner warmth of warmness that comes when a guy knows that he's done his job and pulled the ranch through another dangerous night.

I sat down in front of the overturned Ford hubcap which serves as our dog bowl, and began crunching a few kernels of Co-Op Dog Food. It reminded me of . . . sawdust and the cornbread recipe of certain parties that shall remain monopolis.

Monominous.

Unnamed.

It reminded me of Sally May's cornbread, we might as well come out and say it, and that was no great compliment. Nevertheless a dog has to eat something, so I crunched a few kernels and caught my breath and . . .

Did you hear that? No, probably not because you weren't there, but I heard it: a rattling sound, almost as though something were being rattled.

But what could it be?

Oh. My stomach was growling. Relax. No big . . .

No, by George, there it was again! Yes, a rattling sound, exactly the kind of sound you would expect to hear if something were being rattled. And it wasn't my stomach this time.

Even though I was very tired from all the patrol work, even though I was ready to take it easy for a while, even though I had more or less lost my appetite for adventure—even though all the so-forth, I found myself slipping into the Alert and Readiness Procedures:

—My ears leaped up into Maximum Gathering Mode.

—My tail froze and locked in at a twenty-degree angle.

—I narrowed my eyes and switched over to Infra-red Detection.

—I raised hackles and threw all Hair Lift-up circuits over to Automatic.

—I went straight to Warning Growls and kicked that whole circuit over into Data Control's Master Program.

You probably think all of this took thirty minutes or even an hour. Heh. You'll be shocked to know that I flew through the whole checklist in a matter of SECONDS. That's right, mere seconds. We're talking about blazing speed, fellers.

That's what it takes to be successful in my line of work. Pokey puppies need not apply for this job.

Anyways, once I had reached Full Readiness Mode, I knew that it was time to move out. I shifted into Stealth Crouch Mode and began creeping towards the rattling sound—which, by the way, was getting louder and scarier.

As I drew closer to the mysterious sound, I knew that this was not a simple case of the wind rattling something. By this time my instruments had detected a pattern to the sound, a pattern which indicated that this was not random noise.

It was being created by some type of intelligent life form—or, worse yet, by some unknown Night Monster. Oftentimes the early patterns we get on our instruments look about the same for life forms and monsters.

Which is too bad because if a guy was sure that he was picking up a Night Monster on instruments, he might choose to . . . well, adjust his strategy, so to speak.

I crept forward, on paws that made not even a whisper of sound. *And then, holy smokes, all of a sudden . . .*

C H A P T E R

4

EDDY'S MAGIC TRICK

Okay, you can relax. We had us a little false alarm, is all.

We get those every once in a while. It's no big deal.

See, I had more or less forgotten that Eddy the Rac was in his cage near the machine shed doors. The sounds I had picked up on instruments were the sounds of Eddy rattling his cage.

And let me emphasize that the sound patterns of a coon rattling his cage are almost identical to those created by Unidentified Night Monsters. No kidding, virtually the same, and any dog might have mistaken one for the other.

Which is not to say that I made a mistake. We'd just gotten some, uh, hazy patterns on our . . . I think you get the point.

And it was Eddy the Rac. I greeted this discovery with mixed emotions. On the one hand, a guy can't be too sad about finding a pet coon instead of a Night Monster with flashing red eyes and blood dripping off his fangs. On the other hand . . .

There wasn't much on the other hand, so why don't we just skip it. Finding Eddy the Rac was okay with me, even though I'd gone through all the Readiness Procedures. I wasn't exactly heartbroken.

I took a deep breath, cancelled all the RP's, and sat down. I noticed that my legs were trembling, mostly from excitement.

Eddy was pacing around his cage in that peculiar monkey-walk of his. As you may know, coons resemble monkeys when they walk, because they move both legs on each side at the same time. Does that make sense? Maybe not, but they resemble monkeys.

I watched him. He'd pace for a while, then stop and run his hands over the outline of the cage door. I could hear him muttering to himself.

"Got to get out. Where's the door? Where's the lock? Somewhere. Maybe a hole. There's got to be a hole. Out. I've got to get out."

I had seen all of this before, and I knew that it was just part of Eddy's normal behavior. Around midnight, your average raccoon awakens from sleep and is seized by something called Moonlight Madness.

If he happens to be in a cage, he will spend hours and hours pacing, rattling, probing, and muttering under his breath. This kind of behavior often produces a rattling sound, and as you can see, we had solved that part of the mystery.

After observing Eddy for several minutes, I decided that I might as well reveal my presence. I stood up on all fours and cleared my throat. Eddy froze and turned his beady little eyes in my direction.

"Oh. Hi."

"How's it going, Eddy? You're staying busy, I guess."

"Yeah. Need to get out of here. Can't stand to be cooped up. Don't suppose you could help, could you?"

I chuckled. "Eddy, Eddy! You know the answer to that. Guard dogs aren't allowed to help pet coons escape, period. We've been through this before."

"Yeah. And you helped me before."

"That was an isolated incident, pal. You conned me into letting you out once, and it'll never happen again."

"Twice."

"Okay, twice. You conned me twice, and that makes two reasons why it'll never happen again."

He went back to the business of pacing and probing the cage. I wandered over and watched.

"Eddy, why don't you just relax and enjoy yourself? They'll turn you loose one of these days, and then you'll have to make a living for yourself. You've got a pretty good deal here, room and board and no heavy lifting. What's the problem?"

"Bored."

"So take up singing. Play checkers. Learn some magic tricks."

He stopped. "I do tricks."

"No kidding? Magic tricks?"

"Sure. Want to see?"

"Well . . . sure, why not, as long as they don't take much time. I'm still on Night Patrol, see, and I don't have time for . . . you know some magic tricks, huh?"

"Yeah. Come over here." I went over to a spot directly in front of the cage door. "Sit down." I sat down. "Watch this." I watched.

He reached one of his little hands into the feed bowl and pulled out a kernel of dog food. That's what they were feeding him, see, dog food, the

same stuff we ate. He pulled out one of the ker-nels and held it in the tips of his fingers.

"What's in my hand?"

"A kernel of dog food."

"Now you see it . . ." He brought his hands together, rubbed them around, and threw them out in front of him. " . . . and now you don't."

I stared at his hands. They were open and empty.

"Huh. I'll be derned. How'd you do that?"

"Magic. Want me to bring it back?"

"Well . . . I guess so, sure."

"Now it's gone . . ." He held out his hands and turned them up and down, then reached his left hand behind his left ear. He brought it forward and opened it. " . . . and now it's back. Bingo."

"Say, that's pretty slick, Eddy. I don't know how you did it, but I'll bet you can't do it again. I mean, you've got fast hands but I don't think they're fast enough to fool me twice in a row. Don't forget who's in the Security Business around here."

"Okay. You ready?"

"No, just a second." I moved closer to the cage so that I could study his every move. I knew he was using some kind of trickery and I intended to catch him this time. "Go for it."

He held out his hand, palm-side up. I studied it. Yes, there was a kernel of dog food in his palm. "Now you see it . . ." He brought his hands together, rubbed them around, and threw them into the air. " . . . and now you don't."

"Wait a minute, let me take a good look at those hands." He presented his hands, open and palms-up. By George, they were empty.

No sign of the dog food kernel.

He gave a squeaky little laugh. "Ha. Bet you can't guess where it is."

"Sure I can. It's behind your left ear. You can't fool me, pal, I saw the whole thing."

He bent down so that I could see behind his left ear and . . . hmmm. You might say that it wasn't there, which kind of surprised me.

He grinned. "Guess again?"

"I think not. Let's finish up the trick and go on to something else. Just show me where it is."

"Can't."

"What do you mean, can't? Did you lose it in the mist of the vapors?"

"No. It's outside the cage."

I got a good laugh out of that. "Outside the cage? I don't think so. No way. Sorry."

"Bet me?"

"Bet you? Well, I . . . hey Eddy, I believe my eyes and common sense, and both of them tell me . . ."

"Bet me?"

" . . . both of them tell me that . . . well, betting on duty is a violation of the, uh, Cowdog Code of Conduct, don't you see. In other words, yes, I would love to take you up on your bet, but no, I'm afraid the, uh, regulations don't permit it."

"Too bad."

"But that doesn't mean you can't finish the trick."

He shrugged. "Open the door, I'll finish the trick."

"No problem there."

I pawed at the latches—there were two of them, not just one—until I had them undone. Eddy took it from there, opened the door, and stepped outside.

He took a deep breath of air, looked up at the stars, and said, "Oh, yes!"

"Wait a minute, pal, whoa, hold it, halt. You'd better come up with a kernel of dog food pretty fast or I'm liable to get suspicious."

"Suspicious? Of me?"

"Right. I'm going to suspect that you pulled another cheap con game on me, and if I really thought that was true, Eddy, our friendship would be in trouble. Finish the trick."

"Oh gosh."

"Or bad things will start to happen."

"Oh darn."

I stuck my nose in his face and gave him a growl. "Why you little fraud, I should have known what you were doing. It was just another con job, wasn't it? Huh? Another sneaking, slimy little trick to get you out of the cage, right?"

"What's this?"

"Huh? What's what?"

He reached behind my left ear and held up a
. . . you'll never guess what he held between
two of his fingers. I mean, even I was surprised,
although I had suspected all along that he could
. . . that he might . . .

He held up the missing dog food kernel, you
might say.

"Bingo. Good thing you didn't bet."

"I, uh, yes, I see what you mean, but how did
you do that?"

"Magic. Want it?"

Before I could answer, he flipped the kernel up
into the air, and more or less on instinct, I snapped
and caught it. I chewed it up and swallowed it
down, and by that time Eddy was gone.

I saw him monkey-walking through the snow,
in the general direction of the chicken house. I had
to run to catch up with him.

"Hey, wait a minute. Where do you think you're
going? You're supposed to be back inside your
cage."

"No time for that. Got another deal for you."

WHAT? Another . . .

That's just what I needed, another one of Eddy
the Rac's deals.

CHAPTER
5

THE PERFECT CRIME

I had no idea what sort of "deal" he had in mind,
but I was already starting to worry about it.

I mean, the last couple of "deals" he'd pulled had
gotten me into trouble and had even made me look
silly, if you can believe that. Any time you've got a
loose coon on the place, bad things start to happen.

Yes, I was concerned, but what can you do
about a loose coon? A loose coon is like a genie
with light brown hair that has escaped from its bot-
tle. Once the genie is out, it's hard to put it back
inside the toothpaste tube.

The point is that I didn't have much control over
Eddy, once he had gotten out of his cage. I could
have barked and sounded a General Alarm, but I
didn't see any need for such drastic measures.
Not yet, anyway.

It appeared that my best course of action was to wait and watch and see what kind of mischief Eddy got into—and then remove myself from the scenery of the crime, far, far away, so that I couldn't possibly be blamed for it.

That was a good plan. Or it should have been. How was I supposed to know that he would go inside the chicken house? I never would have dreamed it. I mean, what a crazy thing to do!

On our outfit, if a guy wanted to stir up some real serious heavy-duty trouble, all he had to do was mess around with Sally May's chickens.

We're talking about a Shooting Offense, fellers. When it came to chickens and eggs, Sally May had no mercy and zero sense of humor.

When I saw Eddy stick his head inside the door of the chicken house . . . the little door that the chickens used, not the big one . . . when I saw the so-forth and realized what he had in mind, I tried to stop him.

"Say, Eddy, I don't think I'd . . . Eddy, you'd better stay . . . hey pal, you're fixing to get yourself into more trouble than you ever dreamed of!"

It was too late. He didn't hear me or didn't listen or didn't something, and in a flash he was gone—inside the Forbidden Place.

Well, he'd really done it this time. All I could say
was, "Bye bye, Eddy. It was nice knowing you,"
because I wasn't about to set foot inside that place.

No way. See, I'd been there before and I'd gone
to school, so to speak, on the subject of chickens,
and I sure hated to think of poor little Eddy getting hauled in front of the firing squad. But in
the Real World, we sometimes pay a terrible price
for our mistakes.

And that was too bad because . . . well, Eddy was
new to the place and didn't know all the rules. And
he wasn't a bad guy, really, just a little on the

ornery side and too curious for his own good, and it didn't seem fair that . . .

He might not have even known that it was a chicken house. Had you thought about that? He might have blundered in there thinking that it was a storage shed or something and, oh well, maybe I could save the little stupe before he got in over his head.

And so it was that, against my better judgment, I slipped up the little ramp runway and stuck my head inside the door. Don't worry. I had no intention of going inside. A warning, that's all he would get from me, and that was risky enough.

It was dark inside. I cocked my right ear and listened. Not much there, so I switched over to Smelloradar and . . . whoa, just about blew out the control panel! I had forgotten about the powerful odors that gather inside a chicken house.

Smelloradar is calibrated to pick up the tiniest of odors, don't you see, and there are no tiny odors in a chicken house. Just a lot of big ones, and if you're not careful, they can fry all the circuits in your Smelloradar.

Anyways, so far so good. I knew Eddy was in there somewhere, but at least he hadn't started a riot. As long as that condition held, we had some hope of getting him out and saving his life.

I realized that talking would be risky, but it was a risk I had to take. I whispered . . .

"Eddy?" No answer. "Eddy?" Still no . . .

Holy smokes, all at once there was this horrible masked face right in front of me, and I mean only inches away from the end of my . . .

Okay, it was Eddy. You probably thought it was a Night Monster or a ghost or something. Ha, ha. Even I was fooled there for a second, but just for a second.

Not for long.

Just a brief moment of time, and then the voice of reason prevailed and said, "It's only Eddy." Of course. Who else could it be? It was no big deal, no runaway.

"You called?"

"Right. Eddy, I've come to save you. You don't know where you are."

"Chicken house."

"Well . . . yes, but I'm sure you don't realize what it means to be inside this parchickular ticken house."

"What?"

"Chicken house, this particular chicken house."

"Yeah? Come in. We'll talk."

"Ha, ha. I don't think so, Eddy. See, the whole point of my being here," I squeezed through the little door, "is to get YOU OUT, not to get ME IN. You see what I mean?"

"Sure. Listen. Got a deal. You like eggs?"

I stared at his masked face and wondered if he had actually said what I thought he'd said.

"Are you out of your mind? Listen, bud, you're standing in the most dangerous place in Ochiltree County. I mean, a missile range is like a garden compared to this, because a missile is like a flower compared to Sally May when she's on the rampage."

I got the feeling that he wasn't listening, so I poked him in the chest and whispered louder in his ear.

"Do you hear what I'm saying? You haven't seen Sally May in one of her thermonuclear moments, so you'll have to take my word for it. When she's mad . . . well, listen to this."

It happened that I knew a little song about this very subject, so I did it for him. Here's how it went.

When She's Angry

When she's angry, when she's
   wrathful,
The trees run for cover.
And when she speaks of her
   displeasure,
The mountains hide their faces.

It is not that she's unreasonable.
It is not that she's unkind.
She can be as warm as sunlight,
Soft as flowers on a vine.

But if you summon up her
    displeasure,
Prepare yourself for winds and
    tempests.
For her anger is like a blizzard,
A hurricane, volcano, and tornado.

She despises all injustices,
Inequalities and lies.
And she knows when there is
    wickedness
Just by looking in your eyes.

When she's angry, when she's
    wrathful,
The trees run for cover.
And when she speaks of her
    displeasure,
The mountains hide their faces.

Eddy listened to the song but I wasn't sure that he'd gotten the point. He shrugged his shoulders. "She'll never know."

I stared at the outline of his masked face. It was the face of a bandit or a robber. "What do you mean, *she'll never know?* She knows everything. Knowing is her business."

"Got a plan. Can't miss. Fresh eggs for both of us."

I must admit that the mention of "fresh eggs" caused me to, well, lick my chops, so to speak.

"Eddy, your plan won't work. In the first place, the hens are sitting on their eggs. Did you notice that?"

"Right. They're asleep."

"They're asleep now, but when you reach your cold little hand into a nest, they'll go off like thirty-two burglar alarms."

He shook his head. "Got that covered. No problem."

"In the second place, used eggs leave shells behind. When Sally May comes to gather her morning eggs, she'll find shells. Do you suppose she'll think they're clam shells? Shotgun shells? No. She will know exactly what they are and why they happen to be shells instead of eggs."

"Got that covered too. No problem."

"And then do you know what will happen? She'll pull out her list of Prime Suspects, which will contain two names: mine and mine. No thanks. Let's get out of here."

I started toward the door but Eddy caught me by the collar and pulled me back. "You hungry?"

"No. I'm stuffed, couldn't hold another . . ." At that moment, my stomach growled and my mouth began to water. " . . . bite. In other words, no. Or not very. I've seen hungrier nights." I licked my chops. "Okay, maybe I'm hungry but I'm not crazy."

"This'll work. Magic."

I cut my eyes from side to side. "Explain that."

"Magic. Now you see it, now you don't. Now it's broken, now it's fixed. Now it's shells, now it's an egg. Bingo."

"Wait a minute. Are you trying to tell me . . . magic, huh? I'll be derned. That's one I've never tried. And you can make the shells go back together, is that what you're saying?"

"Right. Easy. No problem."

I licked my chops. "Well, by George, you did okay with the dog food trick. Maybe . . ."

Eddy thrust a finger into the air. "Watch."

With that, he crept to the nearest nest, upon which a big fat hen was sitting—fast asleep. The hen was asleep, not the nest. He rubbed his little raccoon hands together, perhaps to warm them up, and slipped them beneath the sleeping hen. He lifted her out of the nest and set her down in an empty nest nearby.

And I'll be derned, she never even cracked an eye. Those coons could do amazing feats with their hands.

A little humor there. Get it? Feats with their hands? But no kidding aside, they really could do a lot with their hands.

Well, at that point I found my eyes drawn to the six or seven fresh eggs sitting in the . . . mercy, it took a lot of chop-licking to control the flow of . . . and my stomach was growling like crazy by this time, I mean it had been days and days since I'd had a decent meal, and by George . . .

You'll never guess what happened then. Even I was surprised.

C H A P T E R
6

ME? SIT ON THE NEST?

SMACK, SLURP!

Three eggs apiece, is how the, uh, treasure divided itself up, and you can't believe how good they were. Best eggs I'd ever eaten, and what made 'em even better was the fact that nobody would ever know.

I mean, here was the Perfect Crime, made possible by Eddy the Rac's incredible magic skills. What a guy. What a deal.

'Course, I'll have to admit that I was a little surprised when he explained MY part in the deal.

I was feeling very good, see. My tummy was warm and full. We had just pulled off the Perfect Crime of the Century. I didn't have a care in the world.

Then Eddy read the fine print, so to speak, and told me how his magic would put those six eggs back together. I was surprised, to say the least, and I believe my response was, "HUH?"

"Wait a minute, hold it right there. You mean for the magic to work, I have to sit on the nest for two hours? Why can't you sit on it? It's your magic, after all."

He waved one hand through the air. "Right. That's the problem. See, egg magic needs a neutral diode."

"What's a neutral diode?"

"Draws electrical smithereens from the ostensible ether. Won't work with me. Too much magic current. Shells won't knit together."

"Hmm. I hadn't thought of that."

I hadn't thought of it because it was way yonder over my head. I mean, I didn't understand any of that stuff he'd said. The guy must have been a genius.

I thought it over for a moment. "So I just hop into the nest and sit there for a couple of hours, huh? That's all there is to it?"

"Yeah. Then scat. She'll never suspect a thing."

"Well . . . I guess you know what you're doing—speaking of which, what *will* you be doing while I'm dioding the electrical smithereens?"

"Close by. Keeping watch. Checking things."

"I see. And if I should happen to fall asleep—which I won't but just in case I do—you'll be around to wake me up after two hours, right?"

"Right. No problem."

"Hmm. It sounds a little crazy, Eddy, but it just might be crazy enough to work. I'll give it a shot, but if those eggshells haven't gone back together after two hours, I'm going to vanish for a few days."

"Fine."

I sure wouldn't want to be anywhere close by when Sally May discovered the crime, don't you see, 'cause when she's mad, the trees . . ."

" . . . run for cover, I know. Fine."

"It's nothing personal. I mean, I like you Eddy, sort of, and I realize that you're probably a scientific genius, but I'm a pretty shrewd negotiator and I don't make deals unless they're airtight."

"Yeah. You're tough."

I put a paw on his shoulder and looked him right in the eyes. "A guy has to be, Eddy. As you get older and gain a little more experience, you'll realize that life is what we live, and if it weren't for life, this would be a pretty lifeless place." He yawned. "Am I boring you?"

"Oh no. It's late."

"Yes it is, but as I was saying . . . hmmm, I seem to have lost my train of thought. I wanted you to remember something about life."

"I'll remember."

"Do that, Eddy, because it was pretty important. I like to help you younger guys every chance I get."

"Right. Thanks."

"I wish I could remember . . . oh well, better get to work on the eggshells." I hopped up into the nest and settled down upon the . . . yikes, I could hear them crunching beneath the weight of my enormous body. "Eddy, are you certain this will work? Something seems to be crunching down there."

"They do that. At first. The diodic polarity has to reverse."

"Oh, sure. I didn't think of that. Okay, pal, I've got things under control here. Check me in two hours." He waved and ducked out the door and . . . "Hey, Eddy." He stuck his head back inside. "I thought I heard someone laughing."

"Oh no. Me, coughing. Bad cough. Chill in the air."

"Well, you'd better take care of yourself. We just might want to go into the egg business," I gave him a secret wink, "if you know what I mean."

"Got it."

G.L.Holmes

He ducked out again and I settled into the business of knitting the eggshells back together. I figured that if I concentrated extra hard on polarating the diatribes, it might speed up the process.

I sure wanted the process to speed up, if at all possible. I mean, two hours can be a long time.

Two minutes crawled by and I thought I would go nuts! It's very hard for your active minds to adjust to the rhythms of a brainless chicken.

How could they sit there on a nest for hours and days? What did they think about? Probably not much.

Oh boy, this was going to be
　　　　　tough
　　　　　　　fluff
　　　　　　　　　fluffy feathers
　　　　　going to be a tough assignment, and perhaps the hardest part would be trying to stay
　　　　asnork
　　　　　　　mirk snicklefritz
　　　　　　　　Beulah calling my name
lovely brown eyes and flaxen
　　　porkchops
　　　　　　snorking the murgle skiffer
and had to stay awake
　　　awoke
　　　　　　awoken
　　　　　　　　away in the clouds of feathers
rushing to burble the murgle
　　　　mumpus womp ragamuffin
　　　　　　turkey bork asnork . . .

I seemed to be hearing a sound. The sound of footsteps approaching. The crunching of snow.

It must be Beulah. She needed me. Beulah needed me. At last, no more bird dog. "I'm coming, Beulah. I'll save you from the rioting porkchops."

I opened my eyes and . . . HUH?

Perhaps I had dozed. Yes, I'm almost sure I had. Not for long, just a short . . . and yet, something had happened to the darkness of night. It had vanished, so to speak, and turned into the . . . well, the lightness of day.

It was daylight. My goodness, how could that be?

Somehow, through some atmospheric condition that even I didn't understand, somehow the hours between midnight and daylight had *compressed themselves* and passed in just a matter of minutes . . . while I dozed.

How else could you explain it? I knew, and was 100% sure, that I hadn't slept more than a few minutes, because . . . well, sleeping on the job just wasn't something we did in the Security Business.

Yes, this was a rare, a very rare condition of the atmosphere, happens only once or twice every hundred years, when you get a layer of cold air and a layer of warm air and . . .

I suddenly became aware of my surroundings. I blinked my eyes and gazed around. Holy cats, I

was in the chicken house, sitting on . . . sitting on a nest? Impossible. There was no way on earth that a Head of Ranch Security would be . . .

Oops. Okay, the events of the past several hours came tumbling back to my memory.

Eddy.

My good pal Eddy. My business partner Eddy. Eddy the Magical Rac who, it appeared, had not awakened me after two hours, as he had promised, so here I was, sitting on a stupid . . .

He had left me hung out to dry, is what he had done, and it was daylight and it just happened that Sally May usually gathered her eggs at that time of the day, and . . . yikes.

I stood up and looked down into the nest to see if the broken eggs had . . . my head came up very slowly. I cut my eyes from side to side.

Okay, it was all coming clear now. The pieces of the puzzle had finally begun to fall into place.

You remember that crazy story, that wild stupid unbelievable story he'd told me, about how broken eggs will knit back together if a guy sits on the nest for two hours?

Lies, all lies.

I hadn't believed that story, not for one minute, not even for a second, although . . . okay, maybe I'd believed it for a few brief seconds, just long enough to . . .

But the bottom line was that . . . actually, there were several bottom lines, all of which threatened to, uh, shorten my career. Those bottom lines were:

1. Eddy had told me a huge whopper of a lie.
2. I, being a trusting soul, had believed him . . . although not totally and not for very long.
3. I now found myself inside Sally May's chicken house.
4. Sally May's chicken house was a very dangerous place for a dog to be at sunrise.
5. Twenty-two head of Leghorn hens were sitting on their nests, staring at me and just waiting to go off in an explosion of feathers and squawking.
6. And, worst of all, I heard someone coming.

Holy smokes, my goose was cooked!

C H A P T E R
7

SAVED BY MY LITTLE PAL

The footsteps were coming closer. I knew it was Sally May—had to be—and suddenly I was seized by panic and terror.

Cold chills ran down my backbone. My breaths came in short bursts. My heart began to pound like a bass drum.

Fellers, it looked very bad, even hopeless.

See, if I moved or tried to run, the chickens would go off, and just imagine how that would look to Sally May—me running out of a squawking hen house.

But if I didn't move or try to run, she would walk in and find me sitting upon a nestful of . . . well, used eggs, you might say. And naturally, she would never think to pin the blame on the guilty party.

Oh no. She would leap to conclusions and follow the line of superficial evidence which . . . which sure 'nuff led right to my front door, so to speak.

Gulp.

Closer and closer. Crunch. Crunch. The footsteps stopped at the door. Maybe she would . . .

Someone was fingering the latch. My eyes focused on the knob. I froze, didn't even dare to breathe. Maybe she would . . .

The knob turned.

The door swung open. The squeaking of the hinges stabbed the silence.

I tried to swallow but my mouth had gone dry.

A long shadow fell across the floor of the chicken house. It wasn't the shadow of Eddy the Rac or Drover or anyone else I wanted to see at that moment.

It was a human shadow. It was coming inside.

Well, I'd had a pretty good life. I had always hoped it would be a little longer than this, and I really hadn't planned for it to end in a chicken house, but a guy doesn't always get to pick and choose his . . .

A human form appeared in the doorway. I found myself staring into the eyes of . . . Little Alfred?

All the air went out of my body. I almost fainted with joy.

He stared at me with wide eyes and then a grin tugged at one corner of his mouth. "Hankie, what are you doing?"

Well, it did . . . uh, look strange, me sitting on a nest in the . . . in the chicken house. It wasn't the sort of thing a . . . well, a guard dog, a ranch dog would do under . . . uh, normal conditions.

I gave him a big smile and whapped my tail.

He crept over to me. "Are you twying to way an egg?"

Uh . . . no, not exactly. You see, Eddy had told me . . . there was no way I could explain it. All at once I was overwhelmed by the feeling that I had done something REALLY STUPID.

I stood up. The boy's eyes went to the . . . well, to the pile . . . to the collection of . . . to the accumulation, shall we say, of eggshells . . . uh, in the nest below me.

His eyes widened. His mouth fell open. Air rushed into his lungs. He covered his mouth with a hand.

"Hankie! You twied to hatch the eggs and you bwoke 'em!"

I cut my eyes from side to side. Why yes, that's exactly what I had . . . what a clever lad! My goodness, with just a few clues and signs, he had by George pieced the whole thing together.

Yes, sometime in the night I had gotten this wild crazy idea, see, and had wondered . . . I had always wondered if a dog could sit on a chicken's nest and hatch the eggs.

So, uh, I'd tried it. Hopped up on the nest. But darn the luck, I hadn't thought about . . . well, what the weight of a dog would do to a bunch of little bitty eggs, don't you see, and darn the luck, I'd broken them all.

I gave him my most sincere smile and several big wags.

But the important point here, and the point I tried hardest to convey and emphasize, was that THIS WAS NO ORDINARY CASE OF EGG THEFT. The eggs had merely broken, is all.

No kidding. Nobody had eaten them.

The boy whistled under his breath. "If Mom finds out that you sat on her eggs, Hankie, she's gonna be mad."

Yes, I'd thought of that, so . . . uh, what could we do to . . . well, prevent the spread of violence and bloodshed?

He cast slow glances over both shoulders. "She'll be out here pwetty quick. We'd better hide the shells."

Great idea. I, uh, hadn't thought of that, but yes, anything to halt the spread of . . . uh . . . violence and bloodshed and promote peace on the ranch. I was for that 100%.

I hopped out of the nest. While Alfred gathered up all the eggshells and crammed them into his pockets, I turned to the rows of hens sitting on their nests. They were watching us very carefully.

"Hi there," I said with a warm smile. "We had a little accident over here, no big deal, nothing major, just a small mess. We'll have it cleaned up in a second and be on our way. Y'all have a good day now, hear?"

I gave them a wink and a casual wave and backed out the door. Alfred followed and eased the door shut. He held his breath and listened. Two or three hens clucked but that was it.

I almost fainted with relief. Holy smokes, had we dodged a bullet or what? I went straight over to the boy and gave him my biggest, juiciest, most thankful lick on the cheek and ear.

He laughed and pushed me away. "Quit wicking me." Then his face grew solemn and he shook his finger in my face. "Hankie, dogs can't make eggs hatch. Don't do that any more."

He was right. I knew he was right. It had been silly of me to think that I could, uh, hatch out a bunch of eggs. I assured him that it would never happen again.

Never ever. And at that point I began plotting my revenge on Eddy the Rac. He would pay for this.

I headed for his cage. Huh? It was empty. Well, that fit his pattern of sneaky behavior. After luring me into his web of lies and half-truths, now he was afraid to come back and face the roses.

Not a bad idea, actually. Perhaps he knew what kind of roses I had planned to give him: a big one, right on the end of his nose.

I heard Little Alfred coming up behind me. "Uh oh. Eddy's gone. But wook. Twacks in the snow."

I "wooked," so to speak, and sure enough, there was a clear line of raccoon tracks, heading off to the south in the direction of Wolf Creek. "Wet's see if we can find Eddy."

Find Eddy? I wasn't so sure that was a good idea. I mean, Alfred's mom had laws against him taking off on hikes without her permission. And this was January, a month when the weather tended to be cold and unpredictable. February, actually.

On the other hand, I could see certain advantages in being somewhere else when Sally May came out to gather the eggs. Maybe she wouldn't find evidence of broken eggs, but surely she would notice the . . . well, sudden drop in production.

That could lead to hard questions and . . . yes, by George, it was a nice morning for a walk.

Why not? The boy was dressed for the weather—snow boots, gloves, cap, and insulated coveralls—and we would leave a clear trail in the snow. If someone really wanted to find us, they could do it without much trouble.

Slim and Loper fancied themselves to be expert trackers, you know, and following our trail would give them a little exercise and something to brag about.

And besides all that, Alfred didn't ask my opinion. He was already on the trail, and I had to run to catch up with him.

We hiked down the hill behind the house and passed the gas tanks. Drover was there, and would you like to guess what he was doing? Pushing up a long line of Z's. Sleeping his life away. Homesteading his gunnysack.

I called to him as we walked past. "Wake up, Halfstepper. Arise and sing. We're on our way to conquer new worlds and you're about to miss the bus."

He jumped straight up and staggered around in a crazy circle. His eyes were crooked, his ears were crooked. Heck, I think even his nose was crooked. These were all sure and clear signs that the little mutt was still half asleep.

He staggered out to join us. "Oh my gosh, did you see that bus?"

"Bus? No, I didn't see a bus."

"Well, I did, saw it with my own eyes."

"Hmm. That's odd."

"Not really. I've never used anybody else's."

"Anybody else's *what?*"

"Eyes. I always use my own."

"Hmm, yes, of course. So do I."

"You saw it too?"

"I didn't say that, Drover, and stop leaping to conclusions. Let's take this thing one step at a time."

"Yeah, 'cause one step always comes before the next one."

"Exactly. A bus on this ranch? Somehow that doesn't add up."

"Yeah, I never was very good with numbers, but I've got good eyes and they saw it."

"Hmm. Strange. Maybe you'd better give me a description."

"Well, let's see. Big. It was big. Real big."

"Got it. Go on. How about wheels? Did it have wheels?"

"Oh yeah, lots of wheels."

"Numbers, Drover. We need numbers."

"Okay. 37, 13, 68, and 4."

I stared at him. "The number of wheels. On the bus."

"Oh. I thought you just wanted some numbers."

"No. The number of wheels."

"Eight?"

"Yes, but it was cornbread and I almost choked, so that doesn't count. But the eggs were delicious, thanks."

"You're welcome."

At that point we reached the north bank of Wolf Creek, and here we had to suspend my interrogation. Why? Because we had to cross the creek.

Hang on while we cross the creek.

C H A P T E R
8
YIKES! A HAUNTED HOUSE!

Little Alfred, who was serving as the official tracker on this expedition, led us across the creek. Drover and I followed.

I waded through the water. Drover hopped across because . . . well, he doesn't like water. He reminded me of a grasshopper, the way he hopped around.

On the south bank, I returned to the interrogation.

"Let's see, where were we?"

"Counting cornbread. I think."

"No, I said that the cornbread didn't count."

"Yeah, arithmatic is tough."

"Speaking of ticks, I haven't seen any lately."

"No, it's winter."

"Exactly." We walked along in silence. "Nice day."

"Yeah. It's starting to snow again."

"That's true, which explains why all these snowflakes are falling from the sky." Another long silence. "Drover, I have a feeling that something has happened to this conversation."

"I wonder what it could be."

"I'm not sure. I just have this feeling . . . okay, I've got it. We were doing a work-up on the bus." I waited for him to pick it up from there. "You do remember the bus, don't you?"

"Well . . . not really. What bus?"

"The bus, Drover, the bus that came through the ranch just a short while ago."

"I'll be derned. What did it look like?"

"Well, let's see. It had eight wheels, as I recall, and it was big. A huge bus. Red, bright red."

"I'll be derned. Was anybody on it?"

"Hmmm, let's see here. That's an obvious question. Funny how you don't notice those details in the midst of . . . a driver. There must have been a driver, Drover."

"Hello."

"What?"

"Someone called my name."

I stuck my nose in the runt's face and gave him some fangs to look at. "I called your name. Is it possible that your mind had wandered, that you weren't listening to my description of the . . . wait a minute. Why am I describing the bus?"

"Well . . . I don't know."

"YOU'RE the one who saw the stupid bus, so you ought to be the one describing it."

"I'll be derned."

We came to a halt. I stared into the great emptiness of his eyes. "You DID see a bus, didn't you?"

"Well . . . I don't think so. What would a bus be doing out here on the ranch?"

"Drover, sometimes I . . ."

I couldn't find the words to express the scrambled feeling in my head, so I started walking again. I caught up with Little Alfred. I threw myself into the task of following the trail. I had to do something to clear the fog out of my brain.

Here he came, padding along and snapping at an occasional snowflake. "What you doing, Hank?"

"I'm working, Drover, doing my job, following tracks."

"Oh good." He stared down at the trail. "Are those bus tracks?"

My head shot up and I fixed him with a gaze of coldest steel. "Okay, that's it, that's all I can stand.

Drover, I have no choice but to put you on report for the rest of the day. You get three Shame-On-You's and I forbid you ever to say the word bus again."

He hung his head. "Gosh, what if I see one? What will I call it?"

"Call it a sub. That's bus backward."

"What if I see a sub?"

"Call it a tub."

"That doesn't make much sense."

"No, and neither do you, so hush."

G.L. Holmes

We continued along in silence for a full ten seconds. Then he said, "They don't look like sub tracks to me."

"HUSH!"

At last he hushed and I was able to concentrate. I mean, after trying to carry on an intelligent conversation with Drover, I had just about lost all my bearings. And marbles.

Talk to Drover sometime and see if you don't lose your marbles.

He's a very strange dog, and I mean VERY strange.

Where was I? I didn't know where I was—standing at a bus stop, waiting for a submarine, counting cornbread, tracking a washtub, I didn't know what was going on.

Boy!

At last I returned to my senses and began to realize that Little Alfred had led us quite a distance from the house. Not only had we crossed Wolf Creek but we had crossed a barbed wire fence and were now in the Parnells' bull pasture, just east of the Dark Unchanted Forest.

I began to feel uneasy about this. In the first place, Alfred hadn't told his ma where he was going. In the second place, a bull pasture was not my favorite place to be. (It contained bulls, don't you see.) And in the third place, if this snow kept up, it would cover our tracks, and if anything bad happened . . .

Well, you know me. I began to worry. Remember, I'm in charge of kids. Years ago I took the Solemn Cowdog Oath, which included the part ". . . will protect and defend all little children against snakes, monsters, and crawling things."

You know what? I've been known to goof off at times, but on this matter of protecting the kids—hey, there are no days off, no foolishness, no compromise.

I was in charge of Alfred's safety and I was getting a little uneasy. I let him know what I was thinking but he didn't listen.

"Just a wittle more, Hankie. See where the twacks go?"

My eyes followed the line of Eddy's footprints. They went straight to . . . hmm, an old abandoned house. The windows were boarded up, the front door hung open, and the roof above the porch was about to fall down.

It looked pretty creepy, to tell you the truth, and . . . what was that? I'd heard a sound: something banging in the wind. Yes, and there it was again, same sound.

Alfred's eyes were pretty wide by this time. "Do you weckon it's a haunted house, Hankie?"

I . . . uh, tried to ignore the cold chills that began skating down my backbone and went all the way out to the end of my tail.

Haunted house? Well, I sure didn't know about that, and I sure didn't *want* to know about it either. It seemed to me that this would be a very good time to head back to the ranch. I mean, with the snow and everything . . .

Alfred began creeping towards the porch. Well, the boy had nerve, I had to give him that, and since I was in charge of kids, I couldn't just stand there and let him . . .

Have we discussed haunted houses? I don't like 'em, never have. Your average haunted house looks creepy and sounds creepy, but the creepiest part of all is that most haunted houses are HAUNTED, and we're talking about ghosts and skeletons.

And bats. I've got no use for a bat. And spiders and witches and pirates, Egyptian mummies, Frankincense monsters, and all kinds of discombobulated spirits.

Is that any place for a normal healthy dog? No sir, show me a haunted house, fellers, and I'll show you the way home . . . only Little Alfred seemed determined to go inside, and I kind of wished he wouldn't.

He began creeping towards the front porch. What could I do but creep along behind him? But then, all of a sudden and out of nowhere, I heard this . . . this strange whispering voice!

Holy smokes, the hair on my back stood straight up and I whirled around to face . . .

Okay, false alarm. I had more or less forgotten . . .

"Drover, how many times have I told you not to creep up behind me when I'm creeping up on a house?"

"I don't know."

"Well, I don't either, but don't do it. You give me the creeps."

"Yeah, I've got 'em too and I don't like 'em. Hank?"

"What."

"This old leg of mine is starting to hurt. And you know what? I don't like the looks of that house."

"That's fine, Drover. If that house could talk, it would probably say that it doesn't like your looks either. Everything works out for the best."

"I don't want to go in there."

"Great. Stand out here and wait for that bus you were talking about."

"All by myself? Hank, I'm scared. Are you?"

"Ha, ha. Scared? Not at all. You see, Drover . . ."

Yikes! What was that strange screeching noise? All at once I forgot Drover and his foolish fears and whirled around to face the attack of . . .

I ENTER THE HAUNTED HOUSE

Actually, it was just the sound of Little Alfred opening the door. It had squeaky hinges, don't you see, very squeaky hinges, hinges that didn't sound like hinges at all.

They sounded more like . . . I don't know, the screech of an Egyptian mummy or something like that, and I'll admit that my nerves were just a bit on edge, mainly because of Drover.

The little mutt had a childish fear of old houses. Thought they were haunted or something. How silly.

Anyways, Alfred had pulled open the door and now he stuck his head inside. For Drover's sake, I hoped that the boy would take one look around and decide that we could probably spend our time better somewhere else.

I was worried about Drover. Maybe I already said that.

He stuck his head inside the door. Little Alfred did, not Drover. Drover was standing behind me, shivering and moaning. I could hear his teeth clacking.

Alfred looked inside, then his head emerged. "I don't see Eddy. It's too dark and spooky."

Well! That just about wrapped it up, didn't it? I mean, when it's too dark to see, it's time to go, right? I turned myself around and pointed like a compass needle in the direction of . . .

That was odd. The boy wrapped his arms around my chest and picked me up off the ground and . . . HUH? *Started stuffing me into the door that led into that HOUSE FULL OF MONSTERS*!!

Hey, wait a minute! We needed to talk this thing out, make some plans, I mean, it was awfully dark in there and . . .

I wouldn't have supposed that Alfred was stout enough to do that, but he did. And there I was, standing on the brink of the edge of the terrible black darkness and . . . gulp . . .

Alfred spoke to me in a whisper. "You go first, Hankie, and check it out for monstoos, 'cause you're big and tough."

Yeah. You bet. That was me, all right, big and tough and my mouth sure was dry. And the insides of my legs sure were wet. Snow melt, no doubt.

Gulp.

Well, there was nothing for me to do but to mush on and hope for the best. After a minute or two, my eyes began to adjust to the darkness. I looked around.

There was an old table, a wood-burning stove, a broken chair, several Mason jars, a packrat's nest, and a layer of dust on everything, but no Eddy. Now that I could see, I felt somewhat bolder. I took a deep breath and a step forward.

Nothing happened so I took another step. Hey, this was going to be a piece of cake. I couldn't help chuckling at my . . . at Drover's childish and irrational fears of old houses. What was an old house but a house that had gotten old?

I decided to call. I cleared my throat. "Eddy? Eddy the Raccoon? A rescue party has just arrived to take you back to the ranch."

No answer. I called again and listened. Ah ha! I heard the little snipe, or at least the scraping of his claws on the floor upstairs.

He didn't want to go back home, that was the deal. Well, too bad for him and what he wanted. We'd hiked all the way over here, crossed rivers and climbed snowy mountains to find him, and by George we weren't going back without him.

I spotted the old stairs near the east wall. I was feeling pretty sure of myself by now and started up the stairs—even though they did, uh, make a pretty scary groaning noise, and I began to notice that the higher I climbed, the darker it got.

Yes, the loft area turned out to be quite a bit darker than the downstairs. I reached the top stop and stepped.

I reached the stop step and top.

I reached the top step and stopped. I stopped and cocked my ear and listened. Yes, there it was again, a faint scratching sound.

"Eddy, come out. We know you're there. We've come to take you home. Can you hear me?"

Then at last I heard his voice. "Yeah. Over here."

"Fine. We've come to take you home. I'll tell you, in all honesty, that it wasn't my idea. This is Little Alfred's business. If it were up to me, I'd leave you here—you backstabbing, two-timing, con-jobbing little fraud! Did you actually think I was dumb enough to think those eggshells would go back together?"

"You never know."

"Well, I was. You know why? Because I was also dumb enough to trust a coon."

"Yeah. Never trust a coon. I could have told you."

"Then why didn't you?"

"I'm a rat. Dirty rat. They ought to lock me up."

I shook my head in disbelief. "Hey Eddy, we've been through all this before. You WERE locked up. You were safe behind bars, just where you ought to be, but then you couldn't wait to get out."

"Yeah. I know. Moonlight Madness. What a rat."

"What a rat is right. Well, come on and we'll rush you back to your cell."

"Can't."

"What do you mean, can't?"

"Two ghosts, right over there."

HUH?

"Eddy, I think we had a little static on the line. There for a second, I thought you said . . ."

"Two ghosts?"

"Right. But you didn't really say that, did you? An answer of 'no' or 'false' will be just fine, either one, just go ahead and say no."

"Yes. Two ghosts. I'm scared to come out."

I must have had my Back-Down-The-Stairs circuits switched over to automatic, because I found myself backing down the stairs. Quietly but with some haste.

"Oh really? Ghosts, huh? Eh, what do they look like?"

"Black robes with hoods. Phantoms. Grim reapers. Hangmen. Electronic eyes that blink. Help!"

"Yes sir, those are ghosts, all right, and it's sure been nice knowing you, pal. If you ever make it back to the ranch, give us a holler."

"Help! Help!"

Gee whiz, I sure hated to run out on the little guy. Even though he'd pulled several low-down dirty tricks on me, he deserved better than THIS. I mean, what a terrible fate, to be a young orphan coon, left alone in a house full of black-hooded . . . whatever-they-were's.

Hangmans. Black-Hooded Hangmans.

Yes, I felt pretty bad, backing down those stairs and knowing that I was fixing to shoot through that open door and go streaking back to the ranch.

On the other hand, Eddy had walked into this mess on his own four legs, and it appeared that he would have to get himself out the same way.

The important thing is—not that I did nothing to help him, but that I felt pretty bad about doing nothing. Remember: It's the thought that counts.

When I reached the bottom of the stairs, I discovered that Alfred and Drover had come inside. There they were, waiting for me in the darkness and dustiness of the dark, dusty living room—or what used to be a living room.

The boy's eyes were big and round. "What is it, Hankie? Did you find Eddy the Wac?"

Through tail-wags and facial expressions and other communication media, I delivered my report to the boy—and to the saucer-eyed Drover, who was cowering between Alfred's legs.

"Okay, guys, I've got good news and bad news. The good news is that Eddy's up there in the loft, and as far as I can determine, he's all right, just too scared to come out."

Drover's eyes were about to bug out of his head. He'd been hanging on every word. "How come he's scared to come out?"

"Good question, Drover, and that takes us right into the bad news. The bad news is that there are two Black-Hooded Hangmans up there in the loft with him." I heard them both gasp. "Do we have any volunteers to go up there and rescue our old friend Eddy?"

Silence, except for Drover's chattering teeth.

"That's what I thought. In that case, I suggest we . . ."

Suddenly we heard a loud CRASH. Then . . . a long throbbing silence.

I glanced at Alfred. He glanced at Drover, and Drover stared at me with two full moons for eyes.

I coughed. "Guys, we've covered the good news and the bad news. Now to the *real bad* news. The door has just blown shut and we may be trapped in here with whatever that is up there in the loft!"

C H A P T E R

10

THE BLACK-HOODED
HANGMANS IN THE LOFT

A restless wind moaned through the rafters of the old house. A piece of loose tin banged on the roof. Three nervous hearts banged away in their respective bodies.

Yikes, I shouldn't have used that word *bodies*. It sounds too scary and this deal has gotten about as scary as it needs to be, without any talk about . . . well, you know.

Let's back up. Our three hearts were beating, yes, but they had nothing whatsoever to do with bodies or skeletons or ghosts or anything like that. They were just . . . beating. That's what hearts are supposed to do, right?

Yes, ours were whamming around in our chests (not bodies), in our chests . . . okay, we were scared. Even I was scared. Who wouldn't be scared? The door had just slammed shut, the windows were all boarded up, and . . .

Drover was the first to break into sheer panic. He started jumping around and running in cir-

G. L. Holmes

cles. "Oh my gosh, Hank, help, murder, Mayday, my leg!"

Little Alfred had been a brave little explorer up to now, but when Drover fell apart, the boy's lower lip pooched outward and downward and began to quiver.

"I want my mommie. And I want to go home."

I tried to think. My mind was racing. "Alfred, try the door. See if you can open it."

He didn't move. He appeared to be frozen. "I want my mom-meeee!"

"Hey, everybody wants your mommie, but you're the only one of us who can open that door. Alfred, open the dad-blasted door!"

A tear slid down his cheek and, my goodness, his lower lip was pooched out about six inches. "I'm scared of hangmans and I don't wike this pwace . . . AND I WANT MY MOM-MEEEEEE!"

Well, we'd lost him. He was useless. And Drover? You talk about useless! After squeaking and running in circles, he found an old feed sack in the corner and tried to hide under it.

That's right, nosed his way under it so that all you could see of him was his hiney and stub tail sticking up in the air. The little goof.

That left ME to hold our little group together—and, yes, to find some way out of this dangerous turn of events. I had to come up with a plan—real quick.

"Eddy? Eddy, can you hear me?"

Silence. Then I heard this reply, made in a loud, raspy, hacksaw voice. "I can hear you, but I ain't Eddy."

Upon hearing this strange voice, I was almost overcome by a sudden urge to . . . well, run through the wall. Which I tried to do . . . BAM! . . . and which didn't work.

The voice from above spoke again. "What was that loud crash? What's a-going on down there, and who are you?"

I scraped myself off the floor, straightened my nose, and shook the stars out of my head. "I can't tell you what my name is until I find out who you are."

"Huh! Too bad for you, 'cause I ain't talkin'."

"All right, then tell me this. Are you one of the Black-Hooded Hangmans?"

I heard whispering. Then, "Yes, we are Black Hooted Hangmans, we surely are, and we're fixing to start hootin' and hang you from the nearest tree if you don't scram outa here and leave us alone, is what we're a-fixing to do. Are you that little bitty ghost with the mask over his eyes?"

"Why . . . yes, of course. Yes, that's me. How did you know?"

"Well, we know 'cause we seen you a-creepin' around up here in the dark, is how we know, and I can tell you right now that we ain't scared of you, not even a little bit."

"Fine, because I'm not scared of you either." That was a small lie. A big lie, actually, but I had to say something.

"Well, you orta be scared of us. We're tough. We're mean. And we're dangerous, ain't we, son?"

It was then that I heard the voice of the second Black-Hooded Hangman. "Oh y-y-yeah, w-we're t-t-terrible. And m-m-mean."

"There, you see?" said the first one. "That's my boy. He's eight foot tall, weighs four hundred and thirty-five pounds, and looks like a go-rilla. He eats trees and horses and big rocks, and he ain't scared of you, not one bit, are you, son?"

"Uh, w-w-w-well . . ."

"See? I told you, and if you don't go away and leave us alone, I'm just liable to send my boy down there to whip you."

"N-n-now P-pa, w-w-w-wait just a m-m-m-m-m . . . second."

"See? I've got this boy on a chain, a big old heavy log chain, and he's up here just a-lunging against that chain, 'cause he ain't had a bloody fight in two whole days and he's just a-burning up to start a fight with somebody."

"P-p-pa, I w-w-wish you w-w-wouldn't s-say things like that!"

"Hush up. Tell him how big you are."

"I'm r-r-real b-b-big, real big."

"Now tell him how mean you are."

"And I'm r-r-r-r-real m-mean, real mean."

"Good. Now tell him how bad you want to go down there and whip the stuffings out of him."

"Uh okay. And my p-pa s-s-says your m-m-m-momma eats b-b-b-boogers."

Dead silence.

"Son, I did NOT say that, now that ghost is liable to come up here and . . . you ort to be ashamed of yourself for spreading trash and lies about your own daddy, your very own flesh and blood, and you just . . . Mister Ghost, I did NOT say that terrible thing about your dear old mother."

"He d-d-d-did t-too, did too. And h-h-he s-s-said s-she wears d-d-d-dirty sox t-t-too."

"Junior, shame on you for . . . son, you are a-fixing to get your poor old daddy thrashed, is what's fixing to happen!"

By this time I had pretty muchly solved the mystery of the Black-Hooded Hangmans in the loft, and this is really going to surprise you. You'll never guess who those guys were.

See, Eddy the Rac had caught a glimpse of them in the darkness and had reported that they were Black-Hooded Hangmans. That had thrown me off the track for just a few minutes, but not for long. Once I heard them talking, I ran a Voice Scan through Data Control, and when the report came back, it said . . .

Hang on, you'll never believe this. The report said that we had us a couple of *buzzards* up there, and we even had their names. Wallace and Junior.

Are you shocked? Surprised? Heh, heh. Not me. I'd suspected all along that . . . okay, I was a little surprised too.

Anyways, this was a good turn of events. I was feeling a whole lot better about the future, for while two buzzards can make noise and talk a lot of trash, they are fairly harmless birds.

"Okay, guys, it's time for show and tell. I can now reveal that I know your names—not only your names but who you are and what you do for a living. Shall I continue?"

In the gloom, I could barely see Junior's head peek over the loft. "Oh M-m-ister G-ghost? M-m-mister G-g-g . . . P-pa, I can s-s-see h-him now, and h-he ain't a g-g-ghost."

"What do you mean, he ain't a ghost?"

"I m-mean, h-h-he ain't a g-g-ghost, 'cause h-he's a d-d-d-dog."

"A dog? Son, I talked to that ghost myself, and I know for a fact that he ain't a dog."

"Is t-t-too a d-d-dog."

"Is not a dog."

"Is t-t-too a d-d-d-dog. Just l-look for y-yourself, yourself." He gave me a shy smile and waved the tip of his wing. "H-hi there, D-d-doggie."

"How's it going, Junior?"

"Oh w-w-well, w-we c-came here b-because of the s-s-snow s-storm, and w-w-we th-thought we s-s-saw a g-g-g-g-g . . . a ghost."

Wallace's ugly bald head came into view. "Son, that is a ghost in a dog suit, is what that is, and we are still in serious trouble."

"N-n-no. He's our d-d-doggie f-f-friend."

"Our . . ." Wallace craned his neck and squinted his eyes at me. I gave him a little wave. He snapped his head around to Junior. Then he snapped it around to me. Then he puffed himself up and yelled, "Son, that there is a DOG!"

By this time Little Alfred could see the two buzzards up in the choir loft. The tears stopped flow-ing down his cheeks and he even managed a smile.

"Why, it's buzzoods, Hankie, two big old buzzoods!"

"That's right, son, and I hope you'll remember who unhaunted the haunted house and unhooded the Hooded Hangmans. I'm not one to brag and boast, but . . . well, you know your ma and how she gets mad at me, and everyone needs a friend, if you know what I mean."

He nodded and grinned. But then a shadow passed over his face. "Hankie, I miss my mommie. Wet's get Eddy and go home."

"Good idea. Hey, Eddy! Come on out and let's go home. Hurry up, before the snow gets too deep."

Wallace glared down at me. "Who's Eddy? We've got no Eddies up here, just me and Junior, so there's no call for you to be a-yelling about . . ."

Just then Eddy came monkey-walking into view. Wallace stared at him for a moment. His eyes popped open and so did his beak. He jumped backward and flapped his wings.

"Hyah! Go on, git outa . . . Junior, what is that thing that just come walking out of the darkness and . . . son, it's that ghost with the mask and . . . hyah, ghost, hyah!"

Pretty exciting, huh? And you probably think the scary part is over, right? Not quite. Just wait and see what happened when we left the haunted house.

G. L. Holmes

C H A P T E R

11

THIS CHAPTER WILL GIVE YOU THE SHIVERS, NO KIDDING

The old man took cover behind Junior.

"Oh P-p-pa, d-d-don't act s-s-so s-s-silly. H-he's only a l-l-l-little c-coon."

"A cocoon? Son, butterflies come from cocoons, and that is no butterfly. He ain't near big enough and . . . why Junior, that is a raccoon, a cute little old raccoon."

"I t-t-told y-you so."

"And we haven't eat a good wholesome meal in three days, Junior, and . . ." Wallace came waddling out into the open. He wore a crazy grin and was rubbing his wings together. He spoke to me. "Say

95

there, neighbor, I don't reckon y'all might consider a trade for that little old raccoon, would you? We'd have to take him on credit, of course."

"Nope. I'm afraid you guys'll have to stick with dead skunks and smashed rabbits on the road."

"Well, don't you think we can't, Mister Smarty Pants! We've been doing just fine without friends like you, and since you're gonna be so stingy, maybe y'all better just leave our house, right now this very minute. Junior, tell 'em to git out of our house."

Junior shook his head. "P-p-pa, p-please h-h-hush."

Wallace gave him an angry glare. "Junior, did you just tell me to hush?"

"Y-y-yeah."

"All right, fine, I'll hush but you'll be sorry."

And with that, old Wallace crossed his wings over his chest, turned his back on us, and pouted.

Eddy the Rac hurried down the stairs, casting puzzled glances back at Wallace. He went straight to Little Alfred and crawled into his arms. As he passed me, I heard him say, "Weird guy. Take me home. Lock me up. No more roaming for me."

Well, we had just about completed our mission and it was time to head back to the house. Eddy crawled up on the back of Alfred's neck and I called to Mister Hide-Under-The-Sack.

Alfred struggled with the door until he got it open. We were greeted by the cold north wind and a dusting of snow.

"Well, Junior, it was fun. And of course it's always a pleasure to spend a few hours with your old man."

His face burst into a huge grin. "Huh, huh, huh!"

Wallace squawked some kind of tacky reply but I didn't stick around to hear it. I had better things to do than stand around and listen to the complaints of a gripy old buzzard. I'd heard enough already to last me several months.

What a grouch.

I caught up with the other guys and took my position at the front of the line. We needed me out front in the Scout Position, don't you see, because it was snowing pretty hard and our trail back to the house had been covered up.

In that kind of situation, we needed our best tracker and trailblazer out front, and that was . . . well, ME, you might say.

We spread out in a line and marched through the snow: me out front, Little Alfred and Eddy in the middle, and little Mister Scaredy Cat bringing up the rear.

We were the conquering explorers. We had braved the storm, unhaunted the haunted house, and rescued Eddy from a couple of hunger-crazed buzzards, and around here, we call that a pretty good day of ranch work.

Yes sir, we had become famous heroes, and when famous heroes return home from an important mission, they don't just walk or slouch along. They *march*, and we're talking about picking up their feet and marching in step.

Hencely, I passed along the order for the entire column to stay in line, pick up their feet, and march in step. Yes, we looked pretty snappy, marching through the snow, and at that point I figgered we needed to sing "The Famous Heroes Battle-Marching Song."

Do you know it? Maybe not, if you've never been a Famous Hero, but here's how it went.

The Famous Heroes
Battle-Marching Song

We are Famous Heroes, y'all.
(We are Famous Heroes, y'all.)
We are proud and we stand tall.
(We are proud and we stand tall.)

Haunted houses scare us not.
(Haunted houses scare us not.)

Hush your mouth and thanks a lot.
(Hush your mouth and thanks a lot.)

Sound off (Famous).
Sound off (Heroes).
Famous Heroes, one two,
One two . . . three four!

Left, left, left right left.
Left, left, left right left.

(HANK)
We left the ranch in the snow,
You're right!
The girls all cried when we left,
You're right!
We hiked all over the universe and
we're just out of sight,
You're right!

Sound off (Famous).
Sound off (Heroes).
Famous Heroes, one two,
One two . . . three four!

(LITTLE ALFRED)
My mommy's my favowit gal,
You're right!

I know she's going to be pwoud,
You're right!
She'll be my fwiend through thick
    and thin, we always will be tight.
You're right!

Sound off (Famous).
Sound off (Heroes).
Famous Heroes, one two,
One two . . . three four!

(DROVER)
This hero's life is new,
You're right!
It's something I rarely do,
You're right!
And my best friend's a gunnysack,
    it keeps me warm at night
You're right!

Sound off (Famous).
Sound off (Heroes).
Famous Heroes, one two,
One two . . . three four!

(EDDY)
I hardly know what to say,
You're right!

I usually sleep in the day,
You're right.
I'm just a slug 'til midnight comes
    and then I go wild at night,
You're right!

Sound off (Famous).
Sound off (Heroes).
Famous Heroes, one two,
One two . . . three four!

Well, as you can see, it was one of the best marching songs we'd ever come up with on the ranch, just right for a bunch of Famous Heroes going home from a huge success on the field of battle.

Yes, if Beulah had been there, no doubt she would have fallen madly in love with me and forgotten all about her stupid, stick-tailed, spotted, dumb-bunny bird dog friend—Plato. What she saw in that guy, I just didn't know, but . . . oh well.

Too bad she wasn't there to see me in my moment of greatest . . .

"Hank, what's that over there?"

It was Drover. He tore me away from delicious thoughts of my One and Only True Love and brought me back to the present moment, marching through the snow with my comrades.

"What?"

"I thought I saw something up ahead."

I halted the column and went back to the rear. "You thought you saw something up ahead? Well, you probably did, Drover, because there are many things up ahead, such as trees, rocks, shrubs, and snowflakes."

"No, it was something big, with four legs."

"I'm sorry, Drover, but that's impossible. You see, I am in the Scout Position. I am in that position because of my superior . . . Drover, something's happened to your eyes. All at once they look like two fried eggs."

His mouth moved but no words came out. And just then I heard Little Alfred say, "Uh oh, twouble up ahead."

I whirled around and . . .

HUH?

A bull? The neighbors' Jersey bull?

Okay, let's pause here to . . . uh . . . pull a few loose threads together, as they say. See, I had been very busy directing the guys . . . the members of the Famous Heroes Symphonic Chorus, don't you see, and perhaps my attention had also drifted into thoughts of . . . well, Miss Beulah, and . . .

I had more or less forgotten that we were marching across the Parnells' *Bull Pasture*, and what would you expect to find in a bull pasture but a . . . well, a bull?

No big deal.

Okay, maybe it was a bigger deal than you might have supposed, because it was a big bull.

Real big bull.

Monster bull, and have we discussed Jersey bulls? They are famous for their nasty disposition. They love to fight and attack helpless creatures such as your cowdogs, your little boys, and your raccoons.

Yipes.

G.L.Holmes

What lousy luck. We'd almost made it to the fence between the Parnells' and our home pasture. I mean, we could see it up ahead, not more than twenty yards away. The only trouble was that the bull stood between us and the fence.

And, fellers, he appeared to be loading up for an attack. He bellered and shook his horns, lowered his head, and began throwing snow up over his shoulder.

Any one of those symptoms would have been serious. All of them together spelled T-R-O-U-B-L-E.

Drover began to squeak. "Oh my gosh, Hank, what are we going to do?"

"We're going to . . . I don't know what we're going to do, Drover, if you must know the truth."

"Oh my gosh, this leg's killing me! I knew I should have stayed home!"

"Well, go stick your head under a sack."

"I don't have a sack!"

"Go buy one."

"I'm broke!"

"Then maybe you could dry up and let me think."

Just then, as if things weren't bad enough, we heard the voice of an angry ranch wife. All eyes shifted to the north, and yes, standing on the other side of the fence with both hands parked on her waist, was . . . Sally May.

Hmmm. This presented us with a thorny problem. Which was the more dangerous: an angry Sally May or an angry bull?

It was just about a toss-up, seemed to me.

C H A P T E R

12

FAMOUS HEROES
FOR SURE!

"**A**lfred Leroy, where on earth have you been!? I've been worried sick about you. I had to call Viola to come up and watch Molly while I tramped around in the snow for thirty minutes, and young man, someone's been in my chicken house!"

I turned to the boy. "Let's see. According to that verse you sang, she's your 'favorite pal,' right?"

"Uh huh, becept when I'm naughty."

At that point, Sally May stepped over the barbed wire fence and came towards us in a style of walking that I had seen many times before: short steps, fists clenched, and arms pumping at her sides.

I must admit that I hadn't expected her to cross the fence. I mean, the bull was standing right there in plain sight, but she showed no more fear of that bull than if he'd been a hummingbird — which he wasn't.

She stalked right up to the bull, kicked him on the leg with her snow boot, and said, "Scat, you nasty thing! Shoo! Hike!"

And then she breezed past him and zeroed in on us with a pair of eyes that seemed to be on fire. The bull's head shot up and he stared at her in disbelief.

But then he went back to pawing up snow and snorting arrows of steam out of his nostrils. Unless I was badly mistaken, he was taking aim at someone's mommy.

She marched up to us and stopped. In the glare of her eyes, we wilted like so many lettuce leaves on the Fourth of July. I mean, she had a talent for making Famous Heroes look and feel like . . . I don't know what. Famous worms.

"Alfred, where on earth have you been, what on earth have you been doing, child, can't you see that we're having a snowstorm? I just don't . . . how can you . . . sometimes I . . ."

Alfred cut her off. "Hey Mom, I think that bull's fixing to come aftoo us."

She whirled around and turned the Laser Look on Mr. Bull. "You silly bull, go on home. Scat!"

For several throbbing seconds, they glared into each other's burning eyeballs. At that point the bull rumbled and took a step towards us, and it was then that Sally May realized the true dangerousness of our situation.

Slowly, she knelt down on one knee. Her right hand reached out and pulled Little Alfred to her. Her left hand reached out and . . . found my collar? My goodness, she dragged me out from behind . . .

Okay, I had more or less stationed myself behind her. I mean, that seemed a good safe place to be. Not that I was afraid of the alleged bull, you understand, but . . . it just seemed a good place to be, that's all.

And I'll admit that I went to Full Air Brakes and locked down all four legs, but you might say that didn't work and my paws dug little trenches in the snow.

She hauled me out into the open, is what she did, and then she spoke to me in a voice that was soft but very firm. And while she spoke, she never took her eyes off the bull.

"Hank, my child is in danger. Help me now and I'll forgive all your many sins."

Sins? Me? Now wait just a . . . all right, maybe I'd run up a small tab in the Sins Department. Not many, just a few, such as . . . okay, eating eggs in her chicken house, and you know, Little Alfred still had those broken shells in his coat pocket and no doubt she would . . .

I swung my gaze around to the bull and became spaghetti. THAT WAS A HUGE BULL, and she wanted ME to go out and . . .

The Moment of Truth had arrived. She was waiting for an answer. The bull was waiting to see which one of us he would tear to shreds.

Gulp.

You know what made up my mind? It was Sally May herself. I mean, here was your average ranch wife who weighed . . . what? A hundred and twenty-five pounds? And that bull probably weighed a ton, but her first thought was *to protect her child,* not to save herself.

Fellers, I admired that. It was the sort of thing a cowdog would do . . . or hope to do. Heroes come in many shapes and sizes, right? Well, this little ranch mom was handling herself the way heroes are supposed to.

By George, she was an inspiration to me and all at once I didn't care how many times she had screeched at me and accused me of terrible crimes and told me that I stunk.

Me, go out and fight a bull for Sally May? You bet! For that courageous mom, I would put it all on the line, and if things didn't turn out well and I got made into cottage cheese . . . so be it.

That's what cowdogs do. That's why we're a little bit special.

I stood up. Our eyes met. She knew. I knew. She patted me on the head. I gave her a lick on the ear. She didn't want that but she got it anyway.

I mean, sometimes a guy can hold back his emotions and sometimes he can't, and when he's fixing to go into battle, why bother to hold it back?

"Good luck, Hank."

I marched forward. The snow crunched beneath my feet. I could hear the bull's breath roaring in his chest, Drover's teeth chattering, and Little Alfred whispering, "Go get 'im, Hankie, beat the snot out of 'im!"

And I even heard the "Famous Heroes Battle Marching Song."

> We are Famous Heroes, y'all.
> Sally May and I stand tall.
> TNT and dynamite,
> Look out, bull, here comes a fight!

I stiffened my tail, raised all hackles, and went into Stealthy Crouch Mode. The bull answered by shaking his horns, and then he bellered again.

It was so loud, I could almost feel his voice on my face.

I kept moving. Closer and closer. Fifteen yards. Ten yards. Five. I stopped, took a deep breath, and threw a glance back over my shoulder. My friends were huddled in the snow, waiting for me to engage the enemy.

I turned back to the bull, and my goodness, he was so BIG and UGLY! My knees were trembling and I felt my courage slipping away. I switched over to Friendly Wags and tried to smile.

"Hi there, uh, Mister Bull. Nice weather, huh? I mean, if you like snow. Ha, ha. Some like snow and some don't, I suppose, and how do you feel about . . . well, peace treaties and so forth? It seems to me that . . ."

He was on me before I knew it, just as though he had been shot out of a canon. Zoom, wham! He loaded me up on his horns, gave his head a toss, and threw me high in the air.

Well, that answered most of my questions and all at once things became pretty simple. When I hit the ground, he was there waiting for me, and he started working me over with those horns.

Bam! Bam! Oof! Ahh! Ooooooo!

Okay, if that's the way he wanted it, by George I had a couple of tricks saved back. When he made his next pass at me, I put the old Australian Fang Lock on his nose, and he didn't like that, even a little bit.

He bucked. He snorted. He pawed the ground. He bellered and bawled in rage. He tossed his head, and since I was more or less attached to his nose, I went along for the ride. Boy, what a ride! Up and down, around and around.

Out of the corner of my eye, I saw a little white comet streaking off to the north—Drover, no doubt. Then Sally May leaped to her feet, snatched up Little Alfred in her arms, and made a run for the fence.

The G-forces were pressing against my body. My jaws were getting tired. I couldn't hold on much longer. I waited. Watched. Held my breath. Hurry, hurry!

They made it over the fence! They were safe!

And at that point I decided it was time to punch in the Eject and Bail Out procedure. It was pretty simple. I slacked off on the jaw pressure and suddenly I was being air-mailed towards the fence. At that point, all I had to do was Drop Landing Gear and . . .

My landing gear happened to be pointed in the wrong direction, since I was flying upside-down, and the landing turned out to be a little rough.

SPLAT! But the snow softened the blow and I was able to leap to my feet and scramble under the fence, one step ahead of the Jersey Express.

G.L. Holmes

We were both panting for air. We glared at each other across the fence.

"You're just lucky there's a fence between us, pal, or I might . . ." He bellered and I . . . well, went to Escape Speed and streaked back to the house.

It was all over—except for the Post-War Celebrations. A huge crowd was waiting for me when I glided into Headquarters: Drover, Alfred, Eddy the Rac, Sally May, Pete the Barncat, even J.T.

Cluck, the head rooster. Oh yes, and Miss Viola had come out with Baby Molly.

Huge crowd. Brass band. Adoring masses. Smiles, flowers, cheers, blown kisses from the womenfolk. That's what greeted me when I marched up to the yard gate.

Sally May . . . you won't believe this, I didn't either . . . Sally May gave me a huge embrace. Heck, she even pressed her cheek against my left ear! With her other arm, she gathered in Little Alfred and hugged him too and . . .

Crunch!

She stared at the pocket of his coat from whence the, uh, crunching sound had come. Oops. She plunged her hand into the pocket and . . . uh, came out with a handful of . . . eggshells, you might say.

Alfred and I exchanged worried looks. Thoughts of the firing squad flashed across my mind. I began rehearsing my story: "Well, you see, Sally May, there was this . . ."

But you know what? She smiled. Nay, she laughed! And she turned to me and said, "You scamps! I don't even want to know what happened. Just don't do it again."

Yes ma'am! No ma'am. Not me, never again! I was a new dog, a reformed dog. I had taken the Pledge!

G. L. Holmes

And would you believe that, to this very day, I have notched up a PERFECT RECORD and haven't done ONE NAUGHTY THING? Can you believe that?

Neither can I. But I'm working on it.

Honest.

Case closed.

Have you read all of Hank's adventures?
Available in paperback at $6.95:

Also available on cassettes:
Hank the Cowdog's Greatest Hits!